Hello, Family Members,

Learning to read is one of the most important accomplishments of early childhood. **Hello Reader!** books are designed to help children become skilled readers who like to read. Beginning readers learn to read by remembering frequently used words like "the," "is," and "and"; by using phonics skills to decode new words; and by interpreting picture and text clues. These books provide both the stories children enjoy and the structure they need to read fluently and independently. Here are suggestions for helping your child *before*, *during*, and *after* reading:

Before
- Look at the cover and pictures and have your child predict what the story is about.
- Read the story to your child.
- Encourage your child to chime in with familiar words and phrases.
- Echo read with your child by reading a line first and having your child read it after you do.

During
- Have your child think about a word he or she does not recognize right away. Provide hints such as "Let's see if we know the sounds" and "Have we read other words like this one?"
- Encourage your child to use phonics skills to sound out new words.
- Provide the word for your child when more assistance is needed so that he or she does not struggle and the experience of reading with you is a positive one.
- Encourage your child to have fun by reading with a lot of expression . . . like an actor!

After
- Have your child keep lists of interesting and favorite words.
- Encourage your child to read the books over and over again. Have him or her read to brothers, sisters, grandparents, and even teddy bears. Repeated readings develop confidence in young readers.
- Talk about the stories. Ask and answer questions. Share ideas about the funniest and most interesting characters and events in the stories.

I do hope that you and your child enjoy this book.

—Francie Alexander
Reading Specialist,
Scholastic's Learning Ventures

D1311566

To Tracy,
You are all we wished for.
—E.B.

For Katie McSunas,
with a great big hug!
—S.B.

Go to www.scholastic.com for Web site information
on Scholastic authors and illustrators.

ISBN 0-439-20634-0

Text copyright © 2000 by Edward D. Bunting and Anne E. Bunting Family Trust.
Illustrations copyright © 2000 by Steve Björkman.
All rights reserved. Published by Scholastic Inc.
SCHOLASTIC, HELLO READER, CARTWHEEL BOOKS and associated logos
are trademarks and/or registered trademarks of Scholastic Inc.

Library of Congress Cataloging-in-Publication Data available

10 9 8 7 6 5 4 3 2 1   00 01 02 03 04

Printed in the U.S.A.   24
First printing, December 2000

Dear Wish Fairy

by Eve Bunting
Illustrated by Steve Björkman

Hello Reader! — Level 2

SCHOLASTIC INC.

Cartwheel
B·O·O·K·S ®

New York   Toronto   London   Auckland   Sydney
Mexico City   New Delhi   Hong Kong

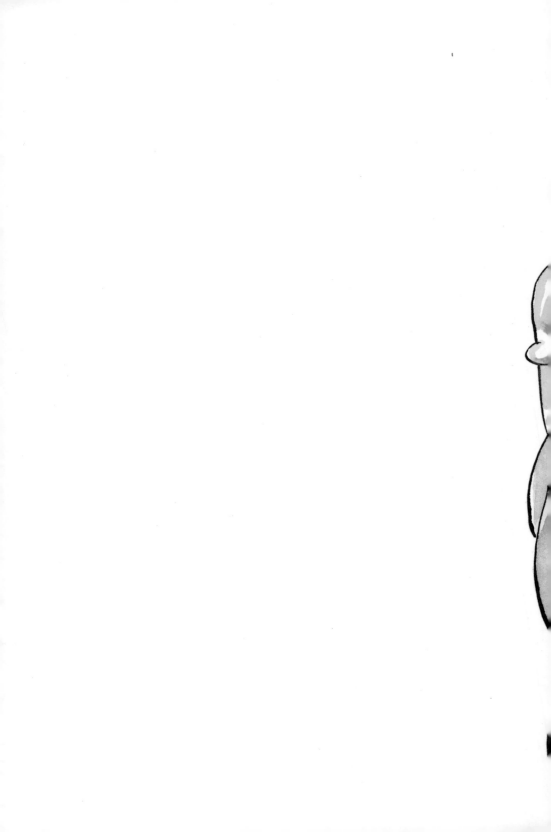

Dear Wish Fairy,

If I had five wishes,
I'd wish for a cat.
His name would be Jim.
I'd be so good to him—

JUST A CAT.

And then, after that,
I would wish for a dog.
We'd play in the park
till the day turned to dark—

JUST A DOG
AND A CAT.

Then I'd wish for a horse.
I think he'd be brown.
I'd ride in my backyard
and all over town—

JUST A HORSE
AND A DOG
AND A CAT.

Then I'd wish for a pig
with a pretty pink snout.
I'd get a pink leash,
and I'd take my pig out—

JUST A PIG
AND A HORSE
AND A DOG
AND A CAT.

If I had five wishes,
I'd wish for a crow.
He'd ride on my shoulder
wherever I go—

JUST A CROW
AND A PIG
AND A HORSE
AND A DOG
AND A CAT
and that's that!

My friends would come over.
I'd share what I got.

If you would come, too,
I'd like it a lot!

So thanks in advance.
I hope you are well.
Gratefully yours . . .

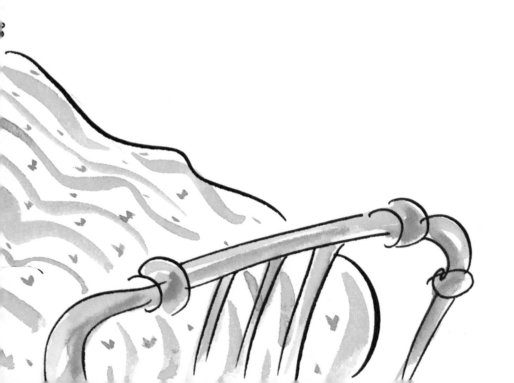

your friend,
Annabel
XOXOXOX